Phoebe
and
Digger

For my darling girls
T. S.

For Sam
J. N.

First edition 2013

Library of Congress Catalog Card Number 2012942614

ISBN 978-0-7636-5281-4

12 13 14 15 16 17 SCP 10 9 8 7 6 5 4 3 2 1

Printed in Humen, Dongguan, China

This book was typeset in Baremo.
The illustrations were done in watercolor, ink, gouache, and permanent marker.

Candlewick Press
99 Dover Street
Somerville, Massachusetts 02144

visit us at www.candlewick.com

Phoebe and Digger

Tricia Springstubb   illustrated by Jeff Newman

CANDLEWICK PRESS

When Mama got a new baby . . .

Phoebe got a new digger.

Mama and the baby were always busy.

So were Phoebe and Digger.

"Waa!" said the baby.

"RMM!" said Digger.

"Urp!" said the baby.

"RMM!" said Digger.

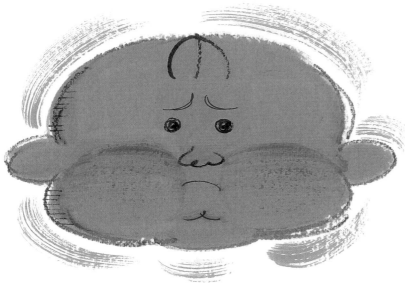 Poop! went the baby.

"RMM!" said Digger.

"I think," said Mama with a sigh, "it is time to go to the park."

Though it took Mama and the baby forever
and a day to get ready . . .

Phoebe and Digger waited very nicely.

Finally, off they went.

Both Phoebe and Digger loved the park.

The park had trees and swings and
a kindly man who sold frozen treats.

But best of all, the park had . . .
real dirt.

Mama and the baby sank onto a boring bench.

Phoebe and Digger went straight to work.

RMM!
Digger built a mountain.

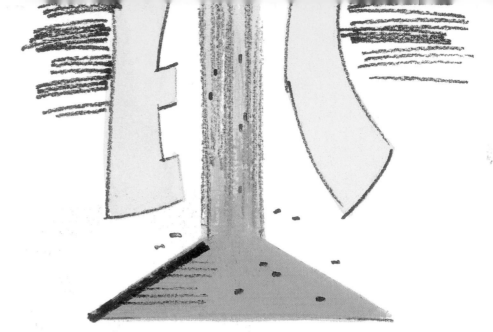

RMM!
Digger knocked that mountain to smithereens.

RMM!
Digger dug up a boa constrictor.

"Eeek!" squealed a crybaby boy.
"Get away! I'm allergic to worms!"

"This is no worm," explained Phoebe.
"This is a dangerous reptile."

Digger rolled closer so the little boy could examine it himself. But instead, he began to wail in terror.

Mama and the baby got involved.

"Be nice!" scolded Mama.
"Phoebe, can't you just play nicely?"

Now the baby began to wail, too. This turned out to be a secret baby signal. Soon every baby in the park was crying.

The noise was deafening.

Phoebe and Digger found themselves sitting
on the boring bench.

With absolutely no frozen treat.

After forever and a day, Mama told Phoebe she
could go play, if she knew how to be nice.

Phoebe and Digger found their own private spot
and got straight to work.

RMM. Digger built a road.

RMM. The town had a castle, with flags on top.

RMM. Also a museum of precious jewels and beautiful flowers.

Suddenly . . .

"COOL DIGGER," boomed a voice.

Phoebe looked up into the face of a big girl with mean teeth.
A girl whose giant hands slowly moved closer, closer . . .

and snatched Digger right away from Phoebe.
"MY TURN," said the giant.

Phoebe tried using her words. "Please give Digger back,"
she said. "I am asking you very nicely."
But the girl paid no attention.

Phoebe tried using her knuckles,
just a little.

Also her foot,
not too hard.

"BACK OFF,
YOU BABY!"

"I'm no baby!"

The girl forced Digger to dig and dump,
scoop and pile. She made Digger go BRR BRR BRR,
a sound Digger absolutely never made.

What could Phoebe do? She'd tried everything she could!
What if she never, ever got Digger back?

Phoebe's eyes grew hot. Her throat itched.
Her shoulders went up and down. Inside her,
something was trying hard to get out.

What could it be?

A **WAA.**

A terrible, achy, throat-burning, eye-prickling,
I'm-all-alone **WAA.**

Just as that **WAA** was about
to burst out of her . . .

"Did you tell that girl she could borrow Digger?" asked Mama. She and the baby were suddenly close by Phoebe's side.

"No," whispered Phoebe.
"I did not."

"Well, then," said Mama.

"ALL DONE." The giant grinned.
She handed Digger back. "THANKS, KID."

Phoebe hugged Digger tight.
Mama hugged Phoebe tight.
Safe! The safest, happiest, best-loved place was where
Phoebe was at this very wonderful moment, a moment
she wished would go on forever and a day.

"Mmm," said Phoebe.

"RMM," went Digger.

"WAA!" said the baby.

Phoebe patted the baby on the head.
This turned out to be a secret sister signal.
All at once, the baby stopped crying.

"Aah," said Mama.

By now it was time to go home.

But first, Mama stopped and bought
a frozen treat from the kindly man.

Phoebe and Mama shared it
as Digger and the baby waited very nicely.